Easter Trumps

This book belongs to:

_____

Easter Bunnies like to hop around
And some Bunnies like to run.
All that jumping up and down
Can give Bunnies a trumpy bum!

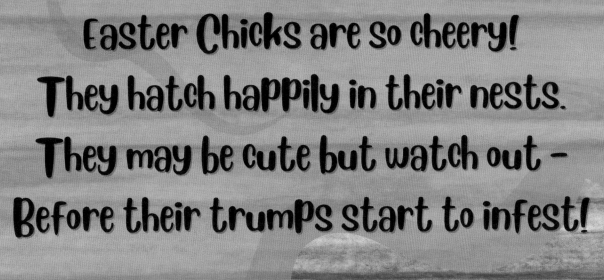

Easter Chicks are so cheery!
They hatch happily in their nests.
They may be cute but watch out –
Before their trumps start to infest!

Another Easter mascot
Is the fluffy Easter Lambs!
You'll find them in an open field
Pumping out all the trumps they can!

For Bunnies, Easter is a busy time
They deliver eggs, far and wide.
But all the hard work that they do
Brings trumps out from inside!

Bunnies love to celebrate.
They like to spread Easter cheer.
But all of that excitement
Can push trumps out from their rear!

Some Bunnies like to hide Easter Eggs
In your back garden or the front!
They leave trumpy clouds behind
While they're planning your Easter Egg Hunt!

Some Bunnies cannot help it -
They trump in their Bunny Pants.
So don't be suprised if you find
A Pong among your Plants!

If you ever get an Easter basket
And you notice a stinky smell,
Have a look for a little Easter chick
Trumping out of it's shell!

Easter Chicks love to celebrate
They have Easter ears that they wear!
The bigger their celebration is,
The bigger the whiff in the air!

Some Easter Chicks like to sit
And smell the Easter flowers.
With every sniff they release a whiff
Due to their trumpy powers!

Easter Lambs are the most trumpy!
They laze and graze all day.
Their trailing trumps fill up the fields –
The smell never goes away!

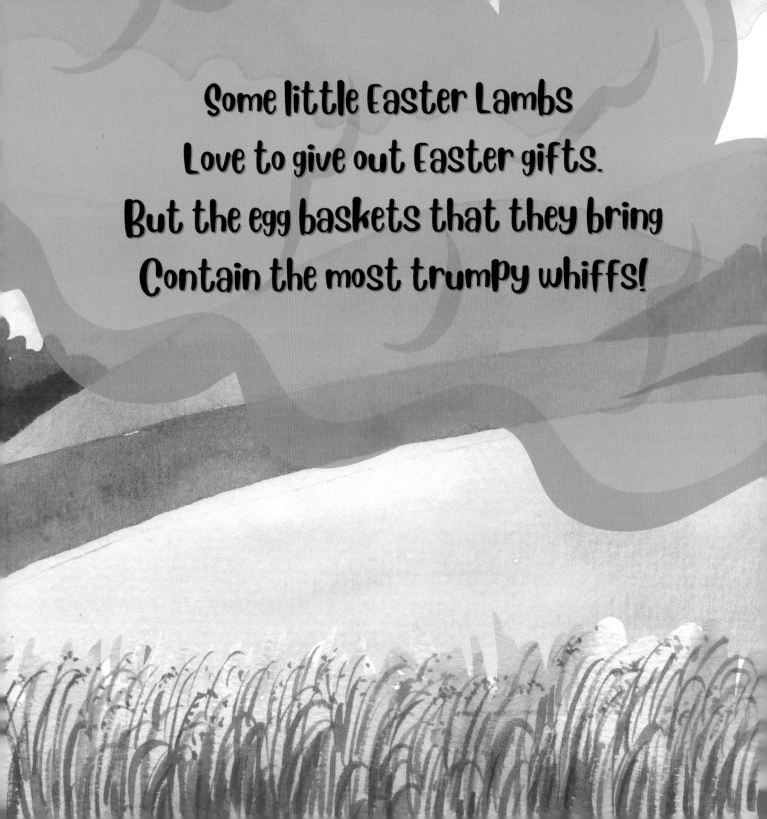

Some little Easter Lambs
Love to give out Easter gifts.
But the egg baskets that they bring
Contain the most trumpy whiffs!

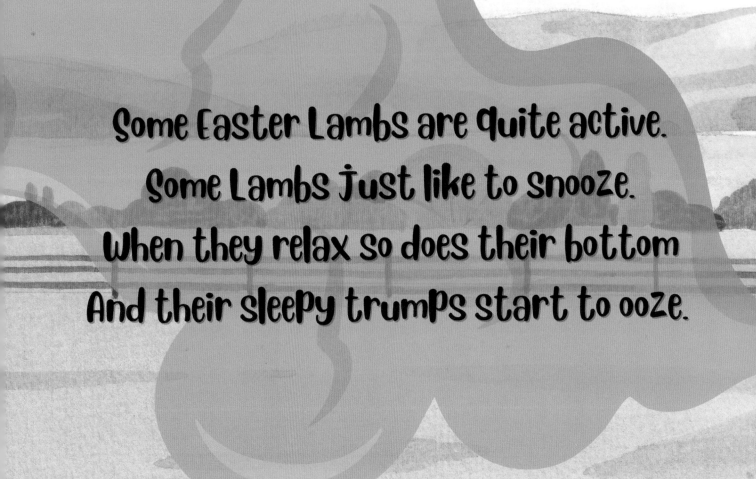

Some Easter Lambs are quite active.
Some Lambs just like to snooze.
When they relax so does their bottom
And their sleepy trumps start to ooze.

Easter friends come in all shapes and sizes.
They're as diverse as they come,
One thing that our Easter friends
have in common
Is a trumpy bum!

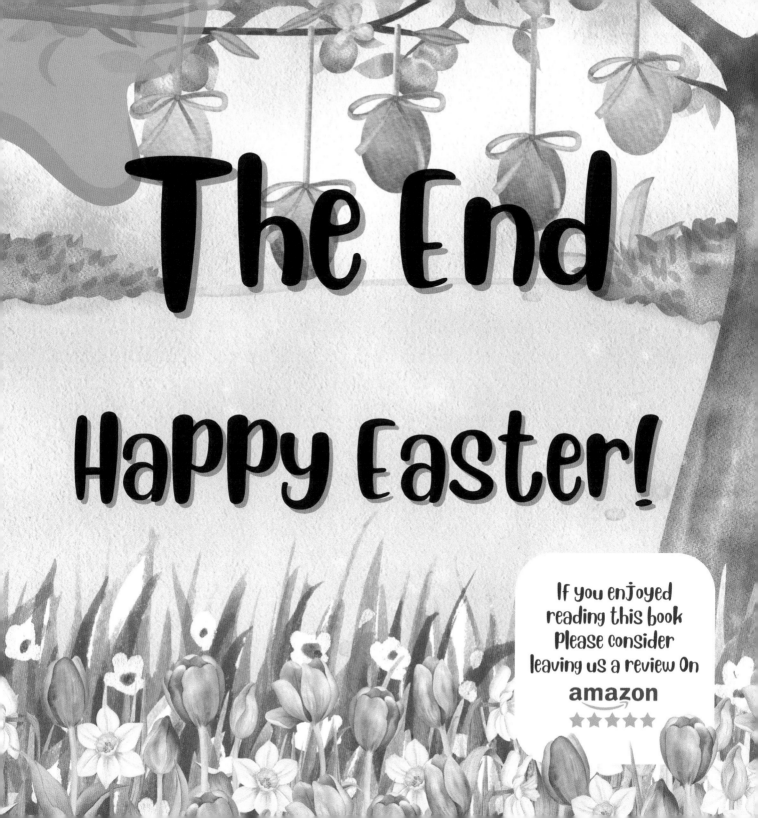

The End

Happy Easter!

If you enjoyed reading this book Please consider leaving us a review On

amazon

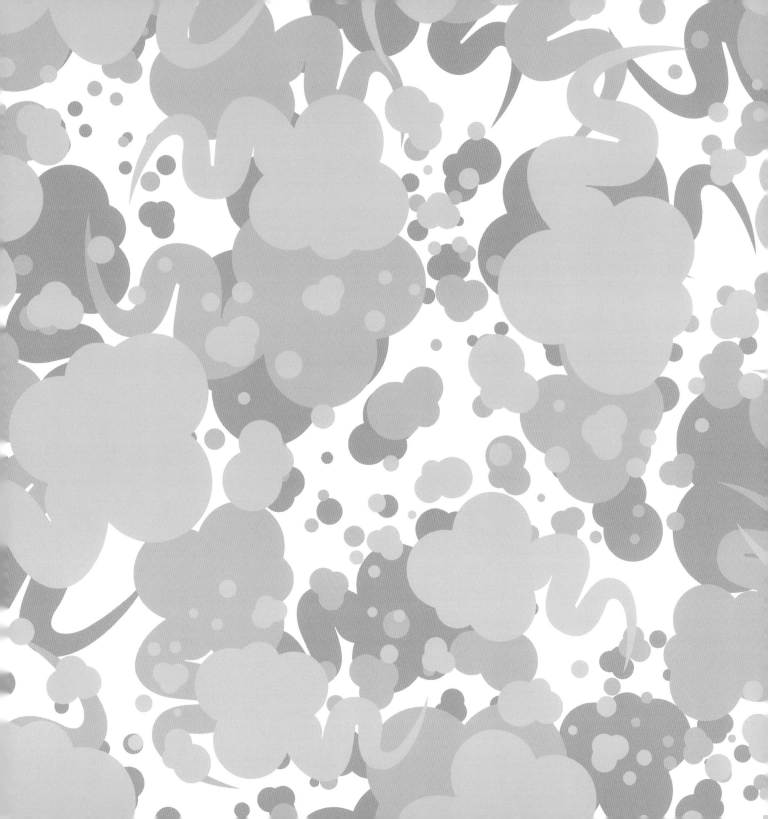

Printed in Great Britain
by Amazon

20082215R00020